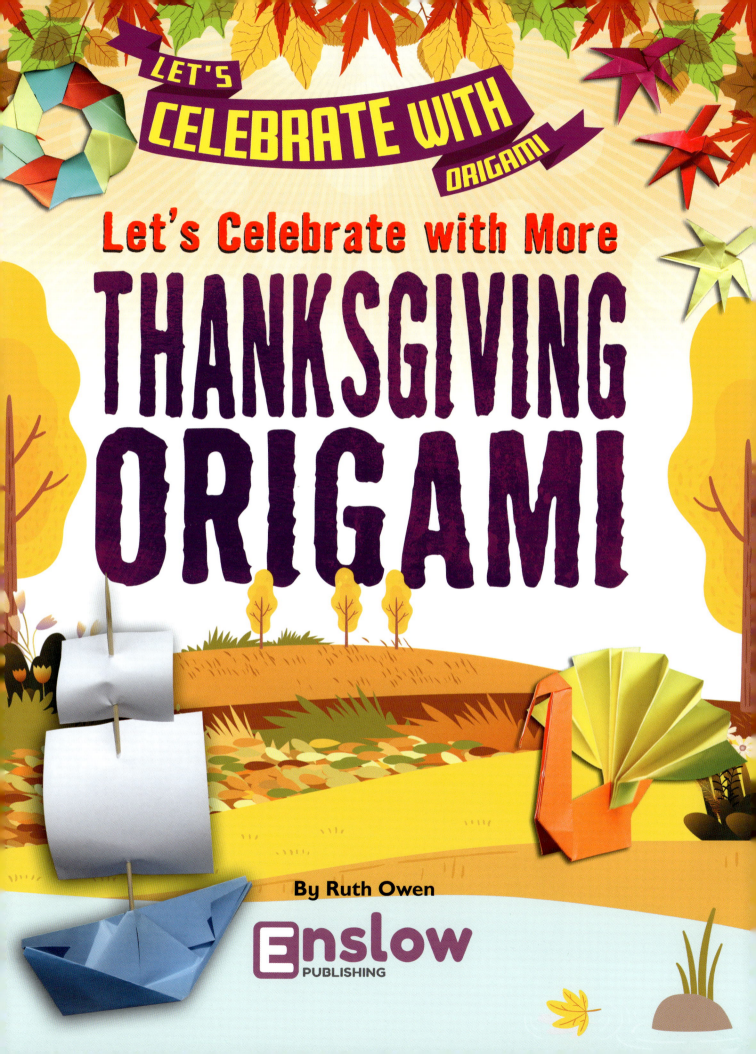

Published in 2022 by Enslow Publishing, LLC
29 East 21st Street
New York, NY 10010

Copyright © 2022 Enslow Publishing, LLC
All rights reserved.

Produced for Rosen by Ruth Owen Books
Designer: Emma Randall
Photos courtesy of Ruth Owen Books and Shutterstock

Cataloging-in-Publication Data

Names: Owen, Ruth.
Title: Let's celebrate with more Thanksgiving origami / Ruth Owen.
Description: New York : Enslow Publishing, 2022. | Series: Let's celebrate with origami | Includes glossary and index.
Identifiers: ISBN 9781978526716 (pbk.) | ISBN 9781978526730 (library bound) | ISBN 9781978526723 (6 pack) | ISBN 9781978526747 (ebook)
Subjects: LCSH: Origami--Juvenile literature. | Thanksgiving decorations--Juvenile literature.
Classification: LCC TT870.O946 2022 | DDC 736'.982--dc23

All rights reserved. No part of this book may be reproduced in any form without permission in writing from the publisher, except by a reviewer.

Manufactured in the United States of America

CPSIA compliance information: Batch #CWENS22: For further information contact Enslow Publishing, New York, New York at 1-800-398-2504

Find us on

An Origami Celebration	4
Origami Tips	6
An Origami *Mayflower*	8
Fold a Turkey	12
Paper Pumpkins	16
Autumn Leaves	20
Fold Some Maple Leaves	24
A Colorful Wreath	28
Glossary, Index, Websites	32

An Origami Celebration

Origami is the art of folding paper to make small **sculptures**, or models. It's the perfect craft for making lovely decorations for the holidays.

Origami gets its name from the Japanese words "ori," which means folding, and "kami," which means paper. People have been making origami models in Japan for hundreds of years.

This book is all about Thanksgiving and is filled with fun origami projects that show you how to make fantastic Thanksgiving decorations—from colorful autumn leaves to a turkey. So let's get ready for the holiday season, and have fun folding!

Origami Tips

Here are some tips that will help you get started on your origami model making.

Tip 1
Read all the instructions carefully and look at the pictures. Make sure you understand what's required before you begin a fold. Don't rush; be patient. Work slowly and carefully.

Tip 2
Folding a piece of paper sounds easy, but it can be tricky to get neat, accurate folds. The more you practice, the easier it becomes.

Tip 3
If an instruction says "crease," make the crease as flat as possible. The flatter the creases, the better the model. You can make a sharp crease by running a plastic ruler along the edge of the paper.

Tip 4
Sometimes, at first, your models may look a little crumpled. Don't give up! The more models you make, the better you will get at folding and creasing.

When it comes to origami, practice makes perfect!

Origami is such good fun that once you get started, you won't be able to stop! With lots of practice it's possible to become very skillful at folding paper and creating models. Keep practicing and you will soon become an origami master.

The origami models on this page have all been made by experienced origami makers. Some of the complicated models are made from many tiny modules, or sections.

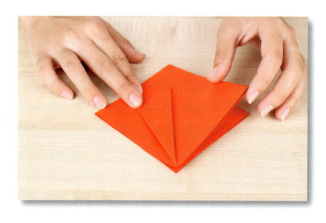

You can even make origami models from money! This butterfly is made from a dollar bill. Money origami is a cool way to give someone a gift of cash.

7

An Origami Mayflower

This first project shows you how to make tiny origami ships using a **traditional** paper boat design.

In 1620, the **Pilgrims** set sail from England in a ship named the *Mayflower*. On their journey to America, the Pilgrims faced many hardships. However, they eventually landed in Plymouth Harbor, in the area that would one day become the state of Massachusetts.

Add masts and sails to your origami ships and you will soon have a fleet of mini *Mayflowers* that can be used as place settings at your family's Thanksgiving dinner.

To make each mini *Mayflower*, you will need:

- A wooden skewer
- One sheet of origami paper (in your choice of color) measuring 6 inches by 6 inches (15 cm x 15 cm)
- Small pieces of white paper
- A black marker
- Scissors
- Glue

(Origami paper is sometimes colored on both sides or white on one side.)

8

STEP 1:
Cut your paper into a rectangle as shown. Place your paper white side down, fold in half, and crease.

STEP 2:
Then fold the paper in half from side to side, but only make a small crease that's about 1 inch (2.5 cm) long.

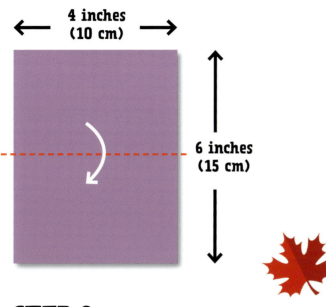

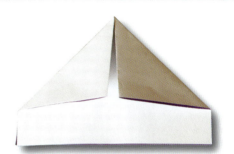

STEP 3:
Now fold the two sides of the model into the center using the small crease you made in step 2 as a guide, and crease well.

STEP 4:
Working with just the top layer of paper, fold up the bottom of the model along the dotted line, and crease. Turn the model over and repeat on the other side.

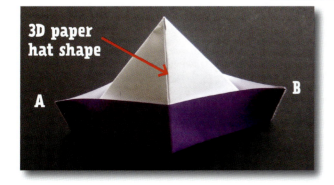

STEP 5:
Now open out the model so it looks like a tiny paper hat. Tidy up points A and B by tucking in the edges of the paper.

STEP 6:
Close up the hat shape by bringing points A and B together, and flatten the model.

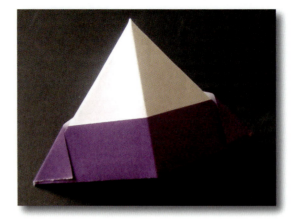

Your model should now look like this.

STEP 7:
Working with the top layer of paper, fold up the bottom of the model along the dotted line, and crease well. Turn the model over and repeat on the other side.

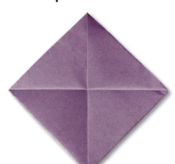

STEP 8:
Now open out the bottom edge of the model to create another paper hat shape.

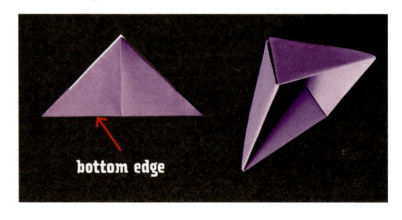

bottom edge

STEP 9:
Now repeat what you did in step 6 by bringing together the two sides of the model and flattening it so it looks like this.

STEP 10:

Take hold of points A and B and gently pull them apart. The model will pop open to create a boat shape.

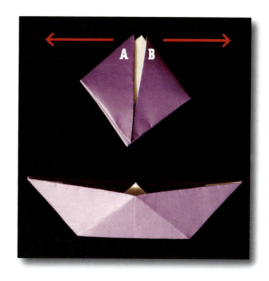

STEP 11:

Open out the bottom of the boat. This will help it stand up.

Your origami model boat is finished.

STEP 12:

To turn your boat into a mini *Mayflower*, cut or snap a wooden skewer in half. Push the pointed end of the skewer through two small pieces of white paper to make the sails. To make a place setting, write a name on one of the sails.

Make a tiny cut in the pointed center section of the boat and slot the skewer into the boat. Add a tiny blob of glue to hold it in place.

Your place setting is complete!

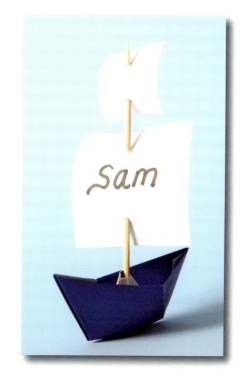

Fold a Turkey

We celebrate Thanksgiving every November with a huge family meal that includes a delicious turkey. But how did this tradition of a celebratory meal get started?

Many of the Pilgrims did not survive their first harsh winter in their new country. But with the help of the native Wampanoag people, the group successfully planted and grew crops in the new year. In the fall of 1621, the Pilgrims had a good **harvest**. To give thanks for this first harvest, the Pilgrims held a feast, and invited their Wampanoag neighbors. This was the first Thanksgiving.

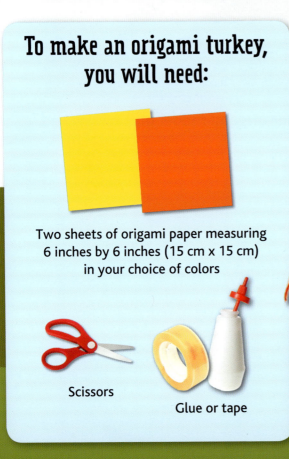

To make an origami turkey, you will need:

Two sheets of origami paper measuring 6 inches by 6 inches (15 cm x 15 cm) in your choice of colors

Scissors

Glue or tape

STEP 1:
Place one sheet of paper colored side down. Fold the paper in half diagonally, crease, and unfold.

STEP 2:
Now fold the two side points in so they meet in the center, and crease well.

STEP 3:
Repeat step 2 by folding both sides of the model into the center again, and crease well.

STEP 4:
Turn the model over. Fold down the top point to meet the bottom of the model, and crease.

Then fold the point back up again to create the turkey's head.

STEP 5:

Now turn the model 90 degrees. Fold the model in half by bringing together points A and B behind the model.

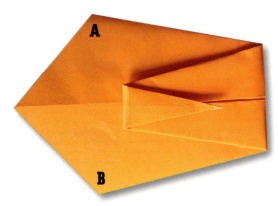

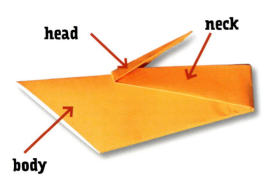

Then, gently pull up the neck part of the model.

STEP 6:

Fold down the point of the turkey's head to make its wobbly wattle.

Cut in here.

Fold in the left-hand side of the turkey's body. Make a small cut into the body that measures about 0.25 inch (0.6 cm). Then unfold.

STEP 7:

To make the turkey's tail, take the second piece of paper and fold it into a series of pleats. Each pleat should be the width of the cut you made in step 6.

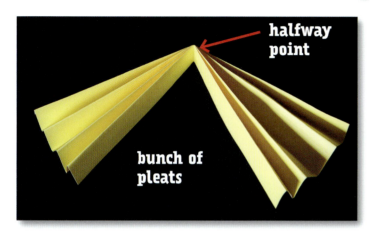

Once all the pleats are made, gather them together into a narrow bunch. Fold the bunch in half lengthwise.

STEP 8:

Now slot the bunch of pleats through the cut you made in step 6, so that half the pleats are on either side of the body. Adjust the length of the cut if you need to.

Your model should now look like this.

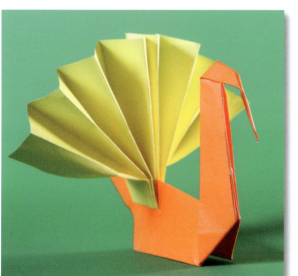

STEP 9:

Fan out the pleats on either side of the turkey's body. Use a little tape or glue to hold the pleats in the perfect position. Your Thanksgiving origami turkey is complete!

15

Paper Pumpkins

It wouldn't be Thanksgiving without pumpkin pie and colorful orange and yellow pumpkins being used as decorations.

The pumpkin is a fruit. In fact, it's the world's largest fruit. Native people in America have been growing pumpkins for over 5,000 years, which makes the pumpkin a truly all-American food.

This Thanksgiving, you can use your origami skills to make some fun paper pumpkins to decorate your home and Thanksgiving dinner table.

To make an origami pumpkin, you will need:

One sheet of orange or yellow origami paper

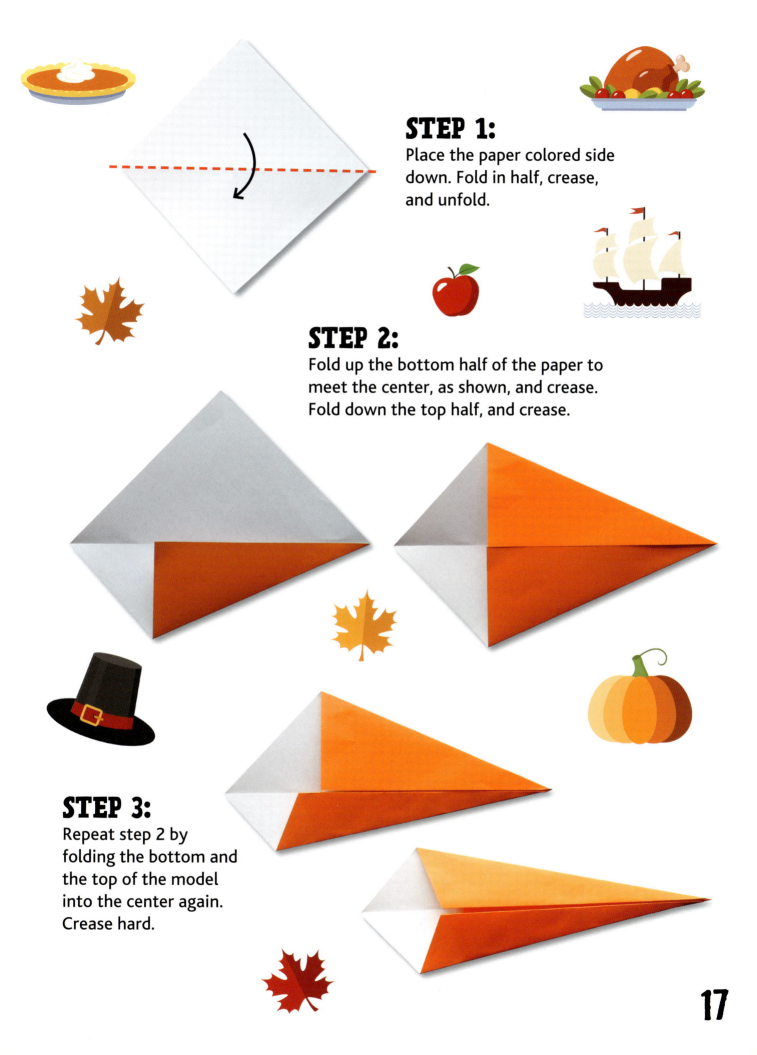

STEP 4:
Fold the bottom and top halves of the model into the center one more time, and crease hard.

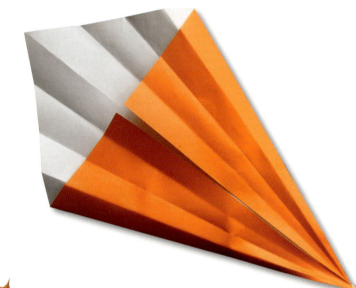

STEP 5:
Unfold the creases you made in steps 3 and 4. Your model should now look like this.

STEP 6:
Turn your model 45 degrees clockwise. Then fold up the bottom point of the model so it meets the top point, and crease.

STEP 7:

Unfold the fold you made in step 6. Now fold down the top point of the model, and crease.

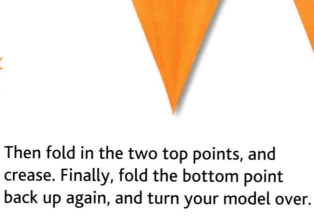

Then fold in the two top points, and crease. Finally, fold the bottom point back up again, and turn your model over.

STEP 8:

To complete your origami pumpkin, twist the top point of the pumpkin to make the stalk.

You can also arrange the creases in the pumpkin to give your model a 3D effect.

twisted stalk

Arrange the creases to make your pumpkin more 3D.

19

Autumn Leaves

When Thanksgiving comes around, fall is already well underway. All around us, trees are getting ready for winter, covering the ground with crunchy yellow, orange, red, and brown leaves.

Fall leaves make wonderful Thanksgiving decorations, and it's simple to make your own paper leaves in warm autumn colors. You can use origami paper or recycled gift-wrapping paper. You can even make some leaves from old brown paper bags. Try making different-sized leaves too.

To make origami leaves, you will need:

Origami paper or recycled paper in your choice of colors

STEP 1:
Place the paper white side down. Fold the paper in half, and crease well.

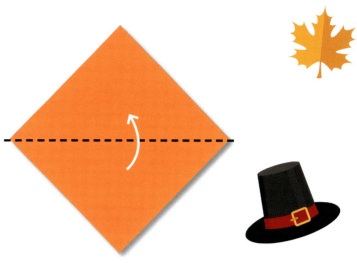

STEP 2:
Working with only the top layer of paper, fold down the top point of the model, and crease.

Turn the model over and repeat on the other side.

STEP 3:
Now fold up the right-hand side of the model along the dotted line, and crease.

Fold the right-hand side of the model back down again along the dotted line so it forms a small pleat, and crease hard.

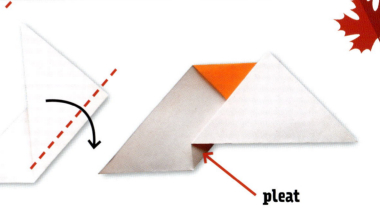

pleat

side A

point

side B

Repeat the folds you've just made and continue pleating the right-hand side of the model until it looks like this.

21

STEP 4:
Turn the model over and position it as shown.

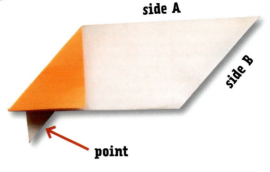

Now fold down the top half of the model along the dotted line, and crease.

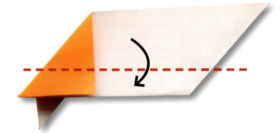

STEP 5:
Fold the bottom edge of the model back up again along the dotted line, and crease.

Your model should now look like this.

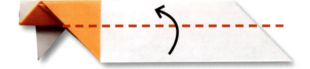

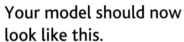

STEP 6:
Now, carefully open out all the pleated folds you've just made until your model looks like this.

22

STEP 7:

Fold up the bottom edge of the model along the dotted line, and crease hard.

STEP 8:

Now, gently open out and flatten your model, but don't unfold the fold you made in step 7. This fold is the leaf's spine.

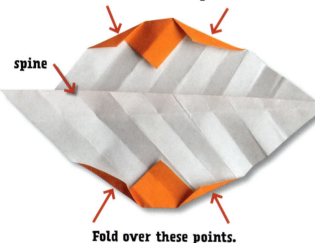

Your model should now look like this. Fold over the two points on each side of the leaf to round off the leaf's edges.

STEP 9:

Turn the model over, and your fall leaf is complete.

23

Fold Some Maple Leaves

This next type of leaf is a little more complicated to make. Follow the steps carefully and you will soon have lots of colorful maple leaves.

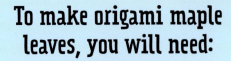

To make origami maple leaves, you will need:

Sheets of origami paper in your choice of fall colors

STEP 1:
Place the paper white side down. Fold the paper diagonally from side to side, crease, and unfold. Then fold from top to bottom, crease, and unfold.

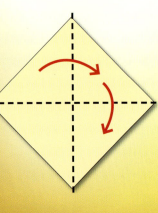

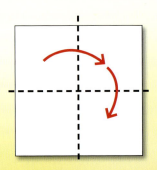

Turn the paper over. Fold the paper from side to side, crease, and unfold. Then fold from top to bottom, crease, and unfold.

STEP 2:

Now, fold and close up the paper by bringing points A and B to meet each other, and point C down to meet point D.

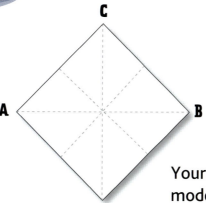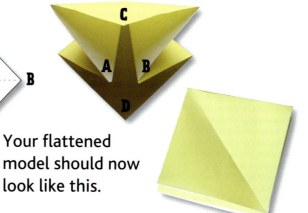

Your flattened model should now look like this.

STEP 3:

Working with just the top layer of paper, fold the two side points into the center, and crease hard.

Then fold down the top point of the model, and crease hard.

STEP 4:

Now, open out the three folds you've just made.

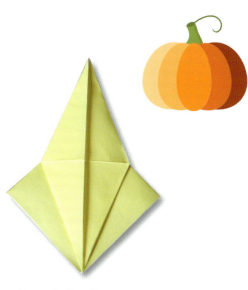

Take hold of point A and gently lift up the top layer of paper. A diamond shape will start to form.

Carefully flatten the diamond shape.

25

STEP 5:

Turn the model over and repeat everything you did in steps 3 and 4.

Your model should now look like this.

STEP 6:

Fold down the top point of the model. Turn the model over, and repeat. Your model should now look like this.

STEP 7:

Fold in the two side points along the dotted lines, and crease.

Turn the model over and repeat. Your model should now look like this.

STEP 8:

Now open out the left-hand side of the model. Gently lift up the left-hand point and then flatten the point and the rest of the model.

Now look at the front face of the model. Working with just the top layer of paper, fold over the right-hand side of the front face, just like turning the page of a book.

Your model should now look like this.

26

STEP 9:
Now open out the left-hand side of the model again. Gently lift up the left-hand point, and then flatten the point and the rest of the model.

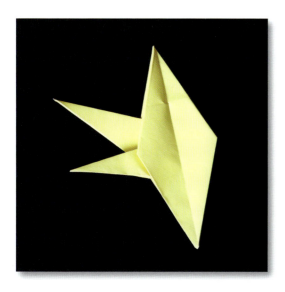

STEP 10:
Fold the right-hand side of the model over to the left, like turning the page of a book.

Then gently lift up the third point, and flatten it.

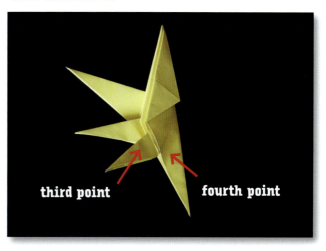

STEP 11:
Finally, fold up the fourth point, and flatten it.

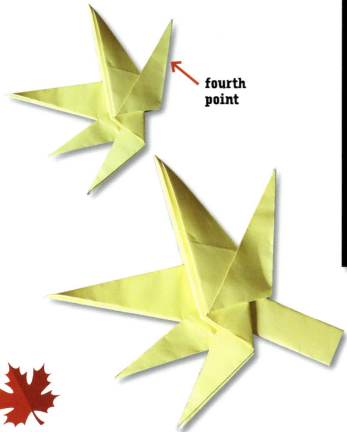

STEP 12:
Take a small square of paper and roll or fold it up to create a stalk.

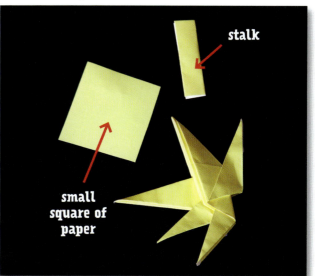

STEP 13:
Glue or tape the stalk to the back of the leaf.

A Colorful Wreath

Holiday wreath decorations can be made from flowers, leaves, fabric—and paper! This final project shows you how to make an origami wreath to decorate a door inside your home at Thanksgiving. It's a modular model, which means it's created from separate sections, or modules.

Use sheets of origami paper to make your wreath, or get creative and use recycled materials such as used gift-wrapping paper and brown paper. Have fun folding, and Happy Thanksgiving!

To make an origami wreath, you will need:

Eight sheets of paper measuring 6 inches by 6 inches (15 x 15 cm) in your choice of colors (this will make a wreath that measures 9 inches (23 cm) across)

STEP 1:

To make one module, place a sheet of paper white side down. Fold the paper in half, and crease.

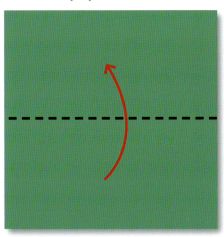

STEP 2:

Fold down the top layer of paper on the right-hand side of the model, crease, and unfold.

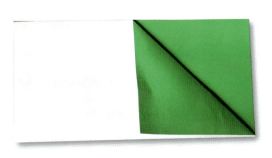

STEP 3:

Now fold down the top layer of paper again along the dotted line, and crease.

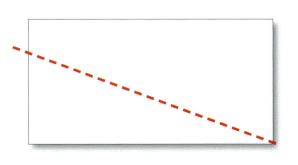

STEP 4:

Turn the model over. Now fold up the right-hand side of the model so that point A meets the top edge.

The right-hand side of the model will slightly rise or roll up.

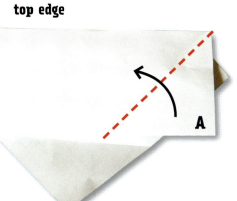

This section will slightly roll up.

29

STEP 5:
Fold down the top left-hand side of the model, and crease.

STEP 6:
Fold up the bottom of the model, and crease.

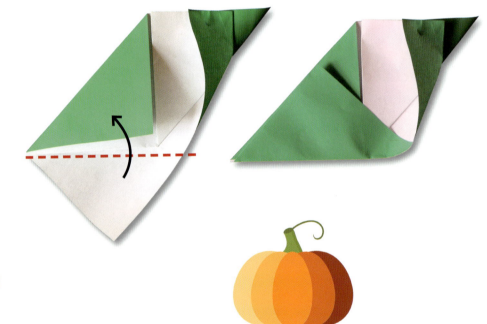

STEP 7:
Turn the model over, and your first module is complete.

STEP 8:
Now make seven more modules.

front of modules

back of modules

To make the wreath, slide one module inside the back of another module as shown.

Continue slotting the modules together, and finally slot module 8 into the back of module 1. For added security, use glue or tape to fix the modules together. Turn the model over, and your wreath is complete.

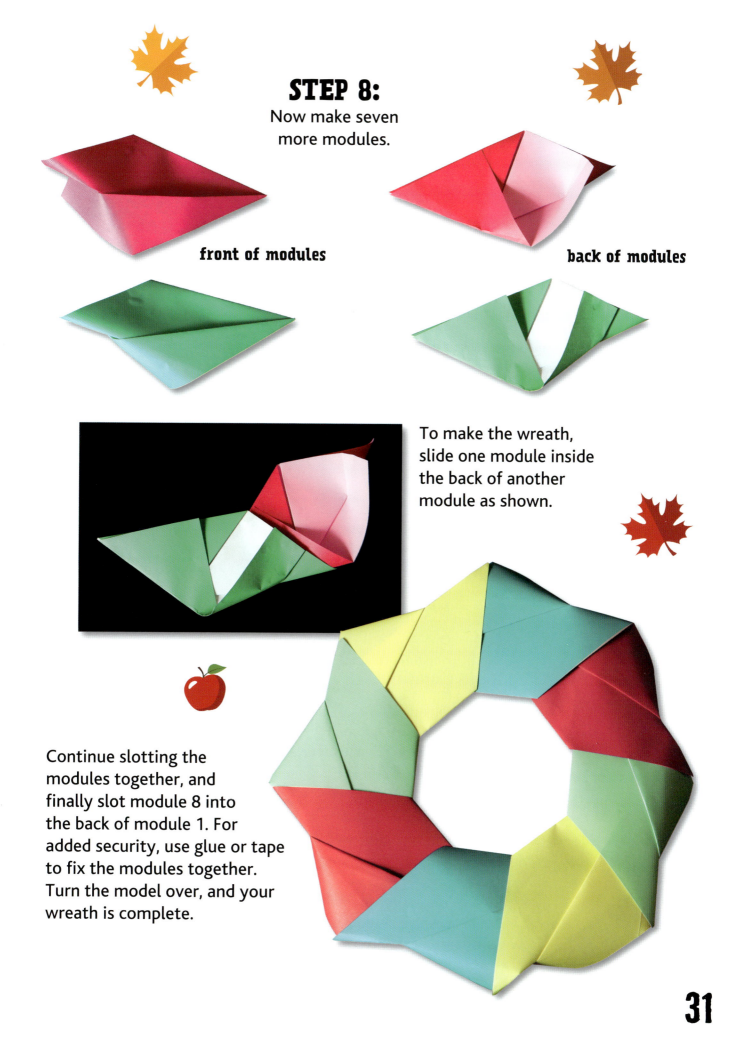

Glossary

harvest
The picking, collecting, or cutting down of fruits, vegetables, and grain crops when they are ripe and ready for eating.

origami
The art of folding paper into decorative shapes or objects.

Pilgrims
Members of a group who came to America from England in search of religious freedom and founded the Plymouth Colony in present-day Massachusetts in 1620.

sculptures
Works of art that have a shape to them, such as statues or carved objects, and may be made of wood, stone, metal, plaster, or even paper.

traditional
Done in a way that has been passed down over time.

Index

A
America, 8
autumn leaves origami model, 20–21, 22–23

E
England, 8

H
harvest, 12

J
Japan, 4

L
leaves, 4, 20, 24, 28

M
maple leaves origami model, 24–25, 26–27
Mayflower origami model, 8–9, 10–11
Mayflower, the, 8

O
origami (general), 4, 6–7

P
Pilgrims, 8, 12
Plymouth Harbor, 8
pumpkin origami model, 16–17, 18–19
pumpkins, 16

T
Thanksgiving dinners, 8, 12, 16
turkey origami model, 12–13, 14–15
turkeys, 4, 12

W
Wampanoag people, 12
wreath origami model, 28–29, 30–31

Websites

www.origami-make.org/howto-origami-thanksgiving.php
www.kids-cooking-activities.com/kids-Thanksgiving-recipes.html
www.weareteachers.com/diy-thanksgiving-crafts/

Publisher's note to educators and parents: Our editors have carefully reviewed these websites to ensure that they are suitable for students. Many websites change frequently, however, and we cannot guarantee that a site's future contents will continue to meet our high standards of quality and educational value. Be advised that students should be closely supervised whenever they access the internet.

32